Violet Victoria

Joanna Weaver
Illustrated by Tony Kenyon

To my daughter Jessica
and her best friend Noelle:
Thank you for always
making room for more friends!

Faith Kids® is an imprint of Cook Communications Ministries,
Colorado Springs, Colorado 80918
Cook Communications, Paris, Ontario
Kingsway Communications, Eastbourne, England

VIOLET VICTORIA
© 2001 by Joanna Weaver for text and Tony Kenyon for illustrations

Editor: Kathy Davis
Graphic Design: Granite Design
First printing, 2001
Printed in Singapore
05 04 03 02 01   5 4 3 2 1

This book belongs to:

_____

"A friend loves you all the time."
Proverbs 17:17 (NCV)

Violet Victoria and Emily Rose
   were best of best friends as everyone knows.
They played every day from morning till night
   then talked 'cross the yard till Mom turned off the light.

Violet loved dress up,
    make-believe, and pretend.
Emily preferred baseball,
    but went along with her friend.

"Darling," Violet would say, sipping make-believe tea,
    "your dress is quite stunning. Now, what about me?"
"My dear Mrs. Diddlehoff," her friend would reply,
    "you're the loveliest of lovely, no one can deny!"

The two were inseparable—two peas in a pod.
　　The thought of more friends seemed incredibly odd.
"Why, who needs another, when I've got you near?"
　　they'd say to each other, then shout out their cheer.

"Forever friends, we always will be.
    Best of best friends, just you and me!"
Then they'd skip, hop and jump, and give a handshake.
    A secret, silly something like a goofy patty-cake.

Then they'd grin, smile, and chuckle,
    as they walked down the street,
repeating the cheer
    to the tap of their feet.

"Can we be your friends?"
other children would say.
"We're afraid not," they'd answer,
then they'd run off to play.

But then came the day when everything changed.
In one single morning their lives rearranged.
It was just after recess, before the big test,
when in walked a girl with a polka-dot vest.

Their teacher said, "Class, this is Katie McGee.
   She's just moved to town from Oakville, Tennessee."
The teacher then whispered in Emily's ear,
   "Will you be Kate's friend? She's lonely 'round here."

Emily stuttered
    then sputtered, "Okay . . ."
But when she looked at her friend,
    Violet just turned away.

"How could you do it?"
Violet cried at recess.
"We agreed no more friends.
Oh, this is a mess!"

But Emily had promised, so she tried hard that week
    to play with them both, although Violet would shriek,
"Forever friends, you said we would be.
    Best of best friends, just you and me!"

Then Violet Victoria with her boa aflutter,
would stalk off the playground, and say with a mutter,
"Some kind of friend Emily turned out to be.
When it came down to choosing, she chose Katie McGee."

Day after day,
    Violet watched from afar
as her former best friend
    became an all-star.

You see, Emily Rose
        loved to bat, hit, and run,
and together with Katie,
        their team always won.

"Who cares?" Violet grumbled.
  "I don't need her," she said.
But inside she felt awful,
  so she bowed down her head.

"Dear Jesus, I'm sorry,"
  Violet prayed with a tear.
"I know that it's selfish
  to hold Emily so near.

"Help me be friendly
   to all that I meet,
and make room for more friends—
   I don't want to compete."

So Violet stopped pouting
    and made up her mind.
She wouldn't be jealous,
    instead she'd be kind.

She began eating lunch
with Emily and Kate,
and found that the new girl
was an awesome playmate.

"I love playing dress-up!
I hear you do too."
Katie grinned, then she asked,
"Wanna play after school?"

"Why, that would be great,"
Violet said, feeling small.
"Could you do something first?
Would you teach me baseball?"

That's how Violet and Emily
and Katie McGee
became best of friends,
as best friends should be.

Though they played every day from morning till night . . .
    Though they talked 'cross their yards
    till Mom turned off the light . . .
These friends learned a lesson we should not ignore:
    God's kind of friendship always makes room for more.

"Can we be your friends?" other children would ask.
"Of course!" the girls said. Then they made it their task

28

to bring kids together, those far and those near,
   till no one was left out when they shouted their cheer.

"Forever friends, everyone—
you and me!

Best of best friends,
'cuz we're God's family."

"Love each other like brothers and sisters."
Romans 12:10 (NCV)

Faith Parenting Guide

Ages: 4-7

Life Issue: My child is learning to be kind
and friendly to others.

Spiritual Building Block: Friendship

Learning Styles

Help your child learn about God's Word in the following ways:

Sight: Ask your child to point to pictures that show Violet's or Emily's friendship. Ask what your child most likes to do with his or her best friend. Explain that sharing is an important part of friendship. Then ask your child to find a picture of Violet not sharing. Point out that when we share our friends, the circle of friendship grows larger, making room for many friends.

Sound: Help your child memorize this Scripture verse, "A friend loves you all the time" (Proverbs 17:17). Then discuss the story.
- When did Violet stop loving Emily Rose?
- Why was Violet jealous of Katie McGee?
- What made her change her attitude?
- How did things get better once Violet made friends with Katie?

Touch: Take some photos of your child with one or two of his or her friends. After the pictures are developed, ask your child to pick his or her favorite shot. Mount the picture on a piece of cardboard or poster board. Write this verse beneath the photo: "Love each other like brothers and sisters" (Romans 12:10). Have your child decorate the "frame"—the area around the photo—using crayons or markers.